Fairground Attraction

Sharon Atkinson

Fairground Attraction

This paperback edition published February 2019

ISBN-13: 9781790118199

Cover via ClipArt

CreateSpace Edition

Also by Sharon Atkinson

From Dreams to Reality

One Last Dance

Beyond Darkness: Deep, Dark & Romantic Poetry

Winter Journal

One Title, Two Minds, Two Stories - In collaboration with Chris Brown

Anthologies

The Perfect Christmas Stuffing

No Sleeves and Short Dresses

Dedication

For Mum & Dad

Chapter 1

Skye stirred restlessly in her sleep as the rain pounded furiously on the window. A clap of thunder awakened her suddenly from a dream. As the storm raged outside bending the trees almost in two, Skye sat up. Switching on her bedside lamp, she took the book of dreams from her bedside table and opened it. It seemed to Skye that every time it rained, she had the same dream. A vivid dream so real she could almost smell the candy floss and hear the music of the rides, along with the screams of excitement.

She shivered, even though her room was quite warm. The dream always began in the same way. She would be standing in the rain at a funfair, watching people enjoying themselves, laughing in delight, as they rode the waltzer. Watching as the neon lights whizzed past her eyes, moving so fast that they all joined together as one. She was always the bystander, watching, waiting, never getting on the ride. It wasn't just the ride she was watching. It was the man, always smiling and laughing along with the punters. The man who collected the tickets and who spun the cars around so fast.

Was this beautiful man watching her too she wondered? He who laughed and joked with the customers, who he twirled round and round. How she wanted to join in their laughter, but as she edged that little bit closer in an attempt to get on the ride, her dream would end and she would be wide awake, listening to the sound of the rain.

Why did the dream man seem so familiar and where had she seen him before? She thought. Had she even seen him before or was the dream so vivid that she only assumed that she had met the stranger before?

She had heard it said many a time that, if you dream the same dream three times it would come true. Skye had this dream more than three times now and still it had not come true for her.

She checked the local papers religiously for news of a fair coming to town. The internet too, but to no avail.

She kept asking herself, who was this dream man? Why did she feel so drawn to him? What was the connection between them? The man was tall and appeared slightly older than her 24 years, she was sure. He had dark shoulder length hair, which curled slightly as it touched the collar of his white shirt. It was opened at the neck revealing a glimpse of his sun kissed skin. His eyes were the colour of sapphires, pulling you in deep. His skin smooth, but with the slightest hint of a shadow on his chin. He had a certain air of mystery to him, which Skye wanted to explore more.

Skye closed her eyes to see the image of this dream man. He was gone. She opened her eyes again and wondered if it was possible to be obsessed with someone who only appeared to her, in her dreams. A man, who in reality, may not exist at all beyond the realms of her subconscious.

Chapter 2

The weeks cruised by. The days were hot and airless and the nights sultry. Skye often walked through the fields, close to her home. Skye worked during the day at the local day-care centre. The children loved her and she had fun making crafts, baking and teaching them new things. Sometimes the children even taught her a thing or two. In the evenings, she worked in a local nightspot as a barmaid, with live bands at the weekends. At work in the evenings, Skye could be herself, let her hair down, relax and listen to the music that she enjoyed.

Some nights whilst walking home across the fields, she could hear what she thought to be, the faint sound of music in the distance and what seemed to be the delicate smell of candy floss tickling at her nose. She knew it was just her imagination and her reoccurring dream playing on her mind.

One Friday evening, her mood was light and carefree as she sang softly to herself when she walked across the field to get home. The full moon that illuminated her way, suddenly disappeared behind a cloud. It made her stop in her tracks and look up into the black velvet night. The first drop of rain splashed onto her face, just to put a downer on her happy mood.

Skye quickened her pace and hoped that the rain would hold off long enough for her to actually make it home, before the heavens opened up completely. The moon appeared again from its hiding place and with her head facing down, she wrapped her arms around her body. Her quickened walking pace became a slight run. Then she heard it. The wind and rain blew past her and seemed to whisper her name.

" Skye."

She stopped and looked around, feeling suddenly scared. The hairs on the back of her neck were standing to attention.

Had it been the wind rustling through the trees, making sounds that sounded like it was calling out her name or had she heard the hushed voice of a man? She turned, peering into the darkness, sensing danger. Her heart skipped a beat as the deep whisper spoke once more. *"I mean you no harm Skye."* This time she knew it was not her imagination or the sound of the wind. The voice sent shivers down her spine. She began to run across the field. Why, oh why, had she not listened to her Grandmother!

"Walking home alone across the field is madness Skye, do you not read the papers. Only last week a young girl was abducted! He left her for dead in the bushes he did. They haven't caught him yet neither, heaven knows what he did to the poor girl!" Her Gran's words, replayed in her head as she ran.

A clap of thunder sounded close and the heavens finally opened up, soaking her to the skin. She ran on, not pausing for anything or anyone. She could see her house now. The light of the porch was burning brightly, illuminating the last few hundred yards to her door and shelter from the rain.

Skye threw open the front door and collapsed in a soggy, wet heap on the floor. Her breathing strained, her new black suede boots ruined from the rain and mud. Kicking them off, she grabbed a towel from the airing cupboard and headed for the bathroom. Turning the shower on, she stepped inside letting the hot water cascade over her tired aching body. It had been a long night; the pub had been busy beyond belief. It was at least ten deep at the bar and didn't ease off, even after last orders was called.

Wrapping a fluffy warm towel around her, she went up the stairs on tip toes, to her room, so she didn't wake her Grandparents. Skye sat down at her desk, and turned on the computer. She sat there for a while, thinking about the voice. How was it at all possible?

Skye thought she may as well check her emails and catch up on her social media before retiring for the night. She sent a quick email to her friend Amber, to organise a girly night out, or a night in with a take away, a film and a good old-fashioned chat. She didn't mention anything about what had happened to her on her way home that night. Skye knew she wouldn't believe her anyway. She wasn't entirely sure she believed it herself. Pressing 'send' she sent the email on its way.

Skye checked through the local events happening over the next few weeks. She was hoping for something unusual hopefully for their 'girly night' out, or the hope that maybe a funfair was possibly coming to town.

There was no mention of any funfairs anywhere in the area. Hardly a surprise, Skye thought.

There was however, an advertisement for a psychic fair. It was to be held in the field, near where she worked and it was going to be there this coming weekend. Funny, she certainly had not remembered any posters or flyers up at work, but to be fair, she was a little engrossed with the band that were playing. She circled the date on the calendar. Was it a coincidence, she wondered, that a psychic fair fell on Midsummer's Day?

Her friends weren't interested in fortune tellers. If she was entirely honest, she wasn't so sure she believed herself, but she had always been fascinated with the whole power of natural magic and the idea of foretelling possible future. Maybe, something will open her mind and she will believe. She figured she could give it a once over just the same. After all, she would hope that they wouldn't tell her something bad or what she didn't want to hear.

Chapter 3

On the Friday evening before the psychic fair, Skye left work, her boss Amanda, wanted to have a little chat.

She wanted Skye to start work at eleven the next morning, as they were going to be very busy. Skye mentioned about wanting to attend the psychic fair, especially as she had never been to one before.

Amanda suggested to Skye that she could pop out for a couple of hours, after she had bottled up and made sure everything was ready for the day. Have an extended lunch break and then look after things at work whilst she herself went and had a look around the fair. Amanda also offered her a nice little bribe of an additional forty pounds on top of her wages and naturally there was always the addition of her tips, especially if the punters were in a generous mood.

Skye agreed to the extra hours, but she knew, the fair would certainly fill the pub with all the extra punters. With the live music planned for the evening they would hopefully continue to party on until the end of the night.

Skye awoke the next morning and stretched in her bed, before jumping up and getting in the shower. As she towel dried her hair, the smell of bacon frying, tickled her nose. Her Grandmother knew how to start the day. She quickly dressed and ran downstairs.

"Morning Gran," Skye said kissing her on the cheek.

"Morning Sunshine. Take a seat, I'll get you a nice cup of tea, then breakfast will be served."

Skye's Gran always liked to do a proper cooked breakfast at the weekends. It was when they all could be together.

Skye cleared the breakfast plates away and left for work. She walked through the field and through the stalls. They were just setting up. The fair didn't open until midday.

Skye was hoping that something would catch her eye as she walked through, so she could return there later. She could feel herself getting excited. Maybe if it had a good turnout, it would become a regular occurrence, she thought.

Skye said that Amanda could go to the fair first as she had not long had a fried breakfast and didn't want her lunch too early. After bottling up and arranging the tables outside the venue, the jukebox was switched on and Skye was ready to open up.

After Amanda had returned, Skye took her break. She had a look round first at the different stalls, selling everything from charms and tarot cards, to crystal balls of all different sizes.

She ended up buying herself a book on tarot reading, which came with a complete deck of Celestial tarot cards. She thought that she could teach herself how to read them. Maybe she could practice on her friends, if they would allow her to. She also purchased some scented candles and some other little bits.

Skye continued to look around the vast array of stalls, with bright colours to entice the customers their way. She suddenly felt strange. Looking around from where she stood, Skye realised she was in the exact same spot as two nights before, when she had heard the voice calling out her name.

She closed her eyes for a moment and listened. Nothing. All she could hear was the excited sounds of the hustle and bustle of those attending the fair.

Chapter 4

Skye still had not decided on what reading to get done, but she felt herself being drawn towards a tent to the right of her. *"Madam Rosa's, Fortunes Told"* was the sign on the outside of the tent. She found herself walking cautiously towards the tent and heard a voice from inside, telling her to enter. Skye parted the thick purple material and walked slowly into the tent. She was apprehensive, but took a seat opposite the lady whom she assumed to be Madam Rosa. The lady spoke.

"Welcome, I am Madam Rosa." She was softly spoken, not what Skye was expecting. Maybe Skye had read too many books or seen too many films, showing the travellers at fairgrounds to appear older than they really were, with their skin well lived in.

"I see you are very special". Madam Rosa reached across the table and took hold of Skye's hands. She closed her eyes, "Yes, very special indeed. I sense a great loss. The loss of loved ones. Possibly your parents?" Madam Rosa opened her eyes and stared straight ahead, like she was looking straight through Skye.

"Your parents want you to know, they are watching over you and they are very proud of you."

Skye's hairs stood up on the nape of her neck. She didn't speak, but tears began to form in her eyes. She swallowed hard, trying to push them away. She did not want to show this complete stranger her weakness.

Madam Rosa continued, "There appears to be a significance around the date, 28th September. I can't see why this date is of relevance to you, but come the day in question, it will all become clear. It is showing me a great prominence in your life."

Madam Rosa freed her hands from Skye's grip and she was now looking right at Skye. Skye stood, a little shaky, but thanked Madam Rosa for her time, getting out her money to pay for the reading. Madam Rosa shook her head, and told her that there would be no charge. She told Skye that she had hardly been able to tell her anything of use and couldn't possibly take any money from her.

Skye thanked her once again and turned to walk back outside, she stopped when Madam Rosa spoke again.

"Have you heard the voice again Skye?" Skye froze and held her breath. She stood there for a second or two before turning back and staring at Madam Rosa. Skye knew she had not told a living soul about the voice she had heard. She was adamant, that she had not even mentioned a word of it to Madam Rosa, including her own name. In fact, Skye had hardly spoken at all, except to thank her for her services.

Skye moved her lips to speak, but no words managed to escape her mouth. Madam Rosa held up her hand, as if telling her not to say anything.

"Everything is fine and you will hear the voice again. This I am sure. Please don't be afraid. It means you no harm, it's just willing you to find *him* and believe me, you will. You must go now, be happy and let your heart guide you in the right direction. Please Skye, do not worry, I will see you again soon". She smiled.

Skye stood outside the tent trying to compose herself and take in what she had just been told. She was a little shaken up. Madam Rosa knew personal things. Skye had never had a reading done before and if she was being completely honest, she was now a little scared, even though Madam Rosa had told her not to be. She was calming with her words, but it was scary that a total stranger could possibly know things about her and her life.

Skye made her way over to the coffee stand. She thought a strong coffee and maybe something sugary would help to calm her nerves before returning to work. Plus, it would give her a chance to go over everything she had just been told. She took out a notebook from her bag and wrote down what she had been told so she wouldn't forget anything. Especially the date that she was told.

Skye sat down at the refreshment stand with her coffee and doughnut, she would buy a sandwich to take back for later as it was going to be a long day. As much as the words were clear, they were not making any sense to her.

Her whole body shuddered as cold shot through her. She didn't know what to believe, but she knew something was on the horizon, and it appeared to be a good thing.

Then as if on cue and as clear as day to her, the voice called out her name.

"Skye."

Nothing else, just the whisper of her name, for only her to hear it seemed. She knew she was not dreaming or imagining it this time. She had just been told, no less than five minutes ago, that she would again hear the voice. Was it too much of a coincidence? She looked around to see if she could see anyone near her that knew her or, could have possibly called out her name. The place was too crowded for her to notice anyone in particular standing out to her.

Skye looked back towards the tent she had not long left and did notice Madam Rosa come out to usher the next person in. She looked over to where Skye was sitting and smiled at her, with a slight nod of the head. It was as if, she too had heard the voice. Skye returned the smile, but then she saw someone in the distance who looked familiar to her. The person appeared to resemble that of her *dream man*.

It looked like he had just left the back of Madam Rosa's tent. She could only see him from the back, but he still looked very familiar to her. He was walking away from the field in a fast pace. He was dressed in light blue jeans and a white shirt, just like she had seen in her dream many times before.

His hair was even shoulder length, but she could just be seeing anybody. She stood up from the table and started to walk towards him, but he was already too far away. She stopped and just continued to watch him disappear into the distance and only when she could no longer see him or the shape of him, she turned and made her way slowly back to work.

She didn't mention anything out of the ordinary to Amanda, she just said that no one stood out to her, but there was also so many to choose from that she did not know who to approach to get an honest and good reading. She showed her what she had bought from some of the stalls. Amanda was excited and told Skye that she had her palm read and that she had been given quite an accurate reading. Amanda also agreed to let Skye practice her tarot reading on her.

Madam Rosa's words kept replaying in Skye's mind for the rest of the day. It was as if someone had told Rosa all about Skye, right up to the last detail. Skye knew that she had never laid eyes on Madam Rosa before. Their paths had never before met, at least she didn't think they had.

Skye walked across the field again that night to get home. The psychic fair had already packed up and disappeared. The field was just an empty space, except for some rubbish that had not been picked up yet. She walked slowly just in case she managed to see the guy from earlier, or more to the point, in case she heard her name being called out.

It was eerily quiet and the only thing she could hear was her own breathing and the light wind brushing past her as she walked home.

Chapter 5

"*CARL*".

The sound of her own voice woke Skye from her slumber. She sat up in bed a little scared, but mainly confused. She leaned over and switched on her bedside lamp. It was then that she realised it was her voice that had called out the random name and had awoken her.

She didn't know where the name had come from or why she had called it out. Skye didn't even know anybody called Carl. She picked up her notebook that was next to her bedside lamp and wrote the single word "*Carl*" in the centre of a blank page.

Skye checked the clock, it was 02.00 and now she was wide awake. She dragged herself out of bed and walked over towards the window. She watched as the raindrops raced each other down the window pane. Then it registered within her mind, every time she had the dream it was not only raining in her dream, but also in reality. She put it down to being a coincidence. Maybe it was the sound of the rain that subconsciously brought her dream on. Too many thoughts were now rolling around in Skye's mind for her to get back to sleep.

Skye left the raindrops to their racing, walked over to her desk and switched on her computer. Whilst the computer warmed up, she went downstairs to the kitchen and made herself a hot chocolate. Hopefully it would help her to get back to sleep.

Because of the ridiculous hour, it meant that none of Skye's friends were awake or online, so she browsed through the local entertainment and her favourite subject; musical gigs and tours. She did notice that there was still no mention of fun fairs on the local websites. There was something however, that made her smile, her favourite band had a concert coming up. There was nothing better than to listen to some live music to take her mind off everything else that was going on.

The nearest concert to her was on August 23rd. Skye booked herself a ticket immediately and made a mental note to book the night off work for it. She knew there was no point asking any of her friends if they wanted to go, they had completely different taste in music to her, which was probably why they were such good friends in the first place. They were the complete opposite. She smiled all to herself once the payment for her ticket had gone through. Then Skye switched the computer off, finished her hot chocolate and went back to bed.

Chapter 6

A few weeks had passed since the psychic fair and Skye was walking home from work taking her usual route through the field. She looked up and noticed how bright and full the moon was. She stopped for a moment to take in its full beauty and smiled all to herself. As Skye put her key into the front door, she heard the voice. His voice.

The soft sensual, but distant whisper of whom she assumed was Carl, *"Skye, I'll be there"*. It sounded like he was standing next to her.

She turned around, slightly confused. There was nobody there, but she knew that even before she had turned. Skye wanted to talk to the voice, but knew it would be silly to talk into thin air. *Who would be there? Where would he be?* she thought to herself, but the questions remained unanswered. She was confused and didn't know what the voice was trying to tell her.

Skye closed the front door behind her and leaned against it taking some deep breaths trying to compose herself. Skye didn't know if she was scared or if she actually welcomed the voice. Had she been working too hard and was she more than just a little over tired? Was she hearing what she wanted to hear? Skye had wanted to hear the voice, his voice. Whichever it was she needed to relax after a hard night at work.

Skye kept repeating the words she had just heard over and over in her mind. If only she knew what they meant.

When she got to her room she put some music on very quietly and lay down on her bed closing her eyes and relaxing to the soothing sounds of her favourite band.

Madam Rosa popped in to her head. She thought if anyone could explain what had just happened to her, it would probably be her. She wished there was a number that she could call, so she could question Madam Rosa for possible answers.

Rosa did say that she would hear the voice again and she had heard it a few times since that day. Skye didn't even have a business card from when she had her reading done. She did a search online but came up with nothing that would help her. The only other thing she could think of was to check to see if there was another psychic fair in the not too distant future. Much to Skye's dismay, the next one was not until late October and it wasn't that close to where she lived. She went to bed feeling just a little bit frustrated with herself more than anything. Nothing seemed to be falling into place for her.

The day of the concert arrived and Skye left pretty early to get there. She wanted to be at the front and nothing was going to stop her. The venue started to fill up and the support band came on singing at the top of their lungs, hoping to get the crowds going ready for the main act.

Skye was excited and enjoying herself. Then just like the first time she had heard the voice call her name, all the hairs on the back of her neck stood to attention. Skye knew she wasn't alone. It was that feeling of being watched. She turned to see if there was anybody that stood out to her in particular. All she could see were the hordes of people facing forward, watching as the supporting band performed on stage.

The sounds of thunder and lightning echoed throughout the concert hall as loud cheers roared. The headlining band were coming out and the atmosphere was electric.

An hour into the show, Skye's heart raced with excitement as her favourite song started to play. She cheered and clapped along with everyone else, singing at the top of her voice. Tears welled up in her eyes as the meaning of the words sunk in. Then out of nowhere, she got this tingling feeling, as if someone was gently kissing her up and down her neck. Skye closed her eyes to embrace the sensation more, the tingling moved from her neck to her lips. Skye opened her eyes expecting to see someone in front of her with their lips pursed, but of course there was no one actually kissing her. It was more like the vibrations of the music pumping through her.

She turned anyway looking behind her, but it was far too dark to notice if there was anybody that she even slightly recognised. She turned back towards the stage to enjoy the rest of the show and tried to ignore that eerie feeling of being watched. Unfortunately, as much as she enjoyed the show, that feeling stayed with her until the end.

After the final song Skye exited quickly so that she didn't miss her last train home. She walked past the queue of people waiting to get their belongings, completely oblivious to who anybody was or what they were doing. She thought to herself that she was glad she had kept her belongings with her and didn't have to join the long queue.

As she walked past the crowds, she could smell a certain fragrance of aftershave mixed with something that smelled like candy floss. She sniffed the air but didn't ponder over it too much. Maybe it was just a coincidence, but what Skye had failed to notice in her rush to exit the building was the guy in the queue, standing talking to his friends.

It was the same guy that she had followed halfway across the field on the day of the psychic fair. The man had not noticed her walk past him either, but he too hadn't seen her close up. He turned around just a bit too late and only saw the back of a girl leaving, which could have been any concert goer.

Skye was still smiling and humming to herself when she put her key in the door. She couldn't believe they sang her favourite song which always seemed to bring tears to her eyes. She also could not shake the sensation that she had felt as the band were singing that particular song.

Skye closed the door behind her and went straight to bed still full of excitement. She didn't sleep for too long as she was woken by a huge thunderstorm outside. It was much needed as the summer days had been very close lately. A good clearing of the air would certainly help with the humidity.

She found it hard to get back to sleep. So, she just lay in bed listening to the sound of the rain as it hit the window pane. She wondered if she would be able to hear a certain voice calling out her name. There was nothing, except the sound of the summer storm.

Chapter 7

For the next four weeks Skye continued her life as normal, going to her day job, walking across the field to her evening job, hoping to see or possibly find her Mr Right waiting for her. She hadn't even had the reoccurring dream during those weeks or heard her *"dream man's"* voice. It had not even rained since the big thunderstorm on that night of the concert.

The only thing Skye could put it down to, was that it was just a dream after all and nothing more. The voice was probably just her subconscious playing tricks with her overworked mind, regardless of what Madam Rosa had told her. Even though Skye had to admit, Madam Rosa had told her things that only Skye would know.

She wondered to herself if it was silly to have believed so much in a dream. Plus, could it possibly have come true for her, even if she believed hard enough. That was the kind of thing that only happened in the movies. The one thing she was pleased about, was the fact that she had never told anyone what Madam Rosa had told her, or about her actual dream. She had kept it to herself and she didn't have to feel embarrassed around her friends. Maybe her friends were right and all this fortune telling mumbo jumbo was rubbish after all.

Skye put on some very low music, so her grandparents didn't have to tell her to turn it down, which they never did anyway and switched on her computer. She checked her emails and one caught her eye immediately.

Subject: Fun Fair!

"Oh. My. Gosh. I check constantly and my friends know before me. Finally! The funfair is coming." Skye said excitedly to herself.

Skye re-read the email and could not believe her eyes. How could she not have known there was a fair and not to mention, in her local town. She checked the events on a regular basis and she hadn't noticed a single thing. The fair was even going to be on the same field where the psychic fair had been held. Had she been walking around with her head in a bucket? It was arriving on Friday evening, but wouldn't be open until the Saturday

Her breaths were coming short and fast and her hands were getting sticky with sweat. She kept reading the words "fair on Sunday" over and over. She sat back in her chair staring at the words on the screen. Her dream immediately popped in to her head along with the image of her "*dream man*", even if it was somewhat blurred.

Could it finally be happening for her? Is her dream actually about to become reality or was she still chasing false hopes? The questions were flying through her mind.

Dreams were just dreams, even if sometimes they do seem so real Skye thought to herself. There was one thing Skye failed to notice and that was the date on Sunday. Sunday was September 28th. The date Madam Rosa told her would have had some significance to her. She had even marked it with a red star on her calendar.

Skye was clock watching and could not wait to finish work on Saturday night. They had been packed to the rafters. The punters were going to the fair, then popping in for a night cap.

She couldn't believe how excited she was and holding onto that little bit of hope again. She had been to plenty of funfairs in her time, but this time was different. She could feel it. It was meant to be and she was meant to be there. She walked home across the field that night after work, just in case she saw what she was looking for. The fair was already closed up and had been for a while. But the smell of hot-dogs and candy floss still lingered in the air.

Skye awoke to a glorious Sunday morning. She could smell bacon cooking downstairs the perfect smell to wake up to, she thought.

Skye was meeting Amber and the gang at 7:30pm that night. She still had quite a few hours to go. She got dressed and decided to take a walk to go and get the papers for her Grandparents. The main reason was to have a quick look around at the fairground in the daylight, she needed to know if there was a waltzer there.

Nothing was open, which she had expected, but there was that distinct smell of hotdogs and candy floss from the night before still faintly in the air. She inhaled deeply and smiled to herself. Even with the sunlight shining down, the empty fair rides looked eerily spooky. Like they were watching her then she found it. The waltzer!

Skye stopped at the steps of the Waltzer. She stood there just staring up at the empty ride. She eventually turned to start walking back home, when she heard the whispered voice, as clear as day say her name.

"Skye."

A shiver went down her spine but there was no one near her. There was no one around at all. She knew there was no one there and that she was not going to get an answer, but she called out to the voice anyway.

"Carl, is that you?"

Skye waited for a reply, but she knew before the four small words had even left her mouth, that she was talking to thin air.

"Can I help you Miss?"

Skye jumped.

The husky voice came from behind where Skye was standing. Skye turned on her heels. Her hopes were slightly dashed when she saw the older gentleman standing there. He was looking at her, like she was from a different planet. She had been standing there talking to herself.

"We open at five today. You'll have to come back then." He continued.

"I'm sorry, I didn't mean to disturb you. I was just having a quick look around. I hope you don't mind".

"Well there's nothing much to see when we're closed, I'm afraid," he said. "Just these here empty rides."

"Of course. I just thought I heard something, so I stopped. I best be on my way; my Grandparents will think I went to print the papers myself. Sorry again."

"No harm done Miss." He tilted his hat, "I'll probably be seeing you tonight. Have a good day." he said with a wink.

"And to you." Skye walked slowly home. She was positive she had heard the voice that time. It was as clear as talking to her Grandmother, but she didn't want to say that to the man she had just been speaking to. He probably already thought she was a few tickets short of a ride, standing there calling out to absolutely no-one.

Skye had a few hours to wait for Amber to arrive. Skye worked out her outfit for the evening. She felt she should wear the same sort of clothes that she saw herself wearing in her dream. Pale blue tight denim jeans with her black waistcoat style top, just for her own reassurance. Maybe a silly idea that her dream man would actually recognise her. That was silly, it was her dream, how could he foresee what she would wear. He still may not even exist.

Chapter 8

For late September, the evening was still quite warm, but Skye still picked up her long black, floor length cardigan. If her dream was to have any reality, then she was expecting some summer rain.

Amber arrived about thirty minutes earlier than planned and they made their way over to meet the rest of their friends. They arrived at the fair and it was already heaving with people. Skye was excited and said the first ride she had to go on was the waltzer. Amber and the others all eagerly agreed and made their way over to the ride.

They only had to queue for a short while before they were allowed on the ride. Skye shared a car with Amber. Each of the cars were spun so fast and the music was playing loud. Unfortunately for Skye, it was not her *"dream man"* spinning the cars. She could not see him, or anyone that looked like him anywhere. Maybe she just had to face the facts that he did not exist, apart from in her imagination.

Next stop was the Ferris wheel. Even though Skye was not good with heights, she didn't want to appear a scaredy cat or unsociable to her friends, especially as they had all gone along with what she had wanted. She took Ambers' hand and held it for the entirety of the ride. When Skye's feet were firmly on the ground, she let out a breath of relief. The group made their way over to their ultimate favourite ride; the ghost train.

The guys loved to try to scare the girls, but if truth be told, they were the ones probably scared. The ride started off slowly, down the rickety tracks. The moment the cart went through the double doors to the horror of delights that lay ahead, Skye got that feeling she was being watched and not by the skeletons that were hanging around the place. This was the same feeling she had got when she went to the concert in back in August. A tingling sensation down her neck, just like being kissed. She tried to look around, but all she could see in the darkened tunnels were the features of the ride, which glowed neon every now and then.

Getting out of the cart at the end, she paused to have a quick look around. Nothing! After the ghost train they decided to get a drink from the refreshment stand. They ordered their drinks and were deciding on what ride to go on next, when the first drops of rain started to fall.

Skye stopped in her tracks. She could hear a certain song playing in the background which was very familiar to her. It was coming from one of the rides. She knew which ride it was coming from. It was the waltzer.

Skye told Amber that she would be back in a minute or two, there was something she just needed to do. Amber offered to go with Skye, but she accepted that Skye needed to do whatever it was on her own. If only to save embarrassment if Skye was wrong.

Skye walked back towards the waltzer and stood there just watching and waiting. There were spots of rain landing upon her face. She was about to move a bit closer but stopped. The whispered voice she had heard so many times, was right behind her. But this time it wasn't just a whisper. It was soft and sensual and it was real. She could feel it, as the words were spoken.

"Are you looking for me Skye?"

Chapter 9

Skye turned slowly to face him.

"It's you. Carl, right?"

"Yes. I'm Carl. Finally we meet. I knew we would find each other."

"You appear to have been trespassing in my dreams for some time. Now finally, I see that you are real after all and it wasn't just my imagination." Skye said, "I honestly thought I was going mad."

"Yes Skye, I am real and you too have been in my dreams". Carl took hold of Skye's hands; the electricity ran through their bodies. Skye looked at Carl, from head to toe. He was dressed just how she had pictured him. His shoulder length, straight dark hair, with his sparkling blue eyes that seemed to melt her to the spot. Skye was completely mesmerised by him. All she could see was him, everything else around her had disappeared.

Skye was stood staring at her dream man. He was real and he was holding both of her hands and looking into her eyes.

Finally finding her voice again, she asked him what his dreams had been about. He told her that in his dream, he could see this girl all alone. She was walking across a field and then she was watching him work, whilst standing in the rain at the foot of the ride. He said that he'd had the dream several times.

Carl told Skye that he had mentioned his own reoccurring dream to his mother. He also told Skye that she had already met his mother, only she didn't know it.

"You would know my mother as Madam Rosa. She told me that you would turn up at the psychic fair, she had seen it with her all seeing eye." he said using his fingers to make the quotation marks. "I was keeping my fingers crossed and hoping that you would attend. I had to see you with my own eyes, to believe that you did exist. I needed to make sure you weren't just a dream. I hope my Mum didn't scare you too much. She told me what she had told you. I am so very sorry for your loss."

Skye went to speak, but Carl continued.

"You see, my dream felt so real, I had to ask her for help and guidance. I needed the help for me to understand what I was seeing and it got worse when I suddenly heard your voice call out of my name out of nowhere. That scared me the most."

"I felt the same." replied Skye. "It was you, walking across the field the day of the psychic fair. I just wish I had seen you close up and not just from the back. It was making me doubt in my mind that you existed. From the distance you could have been anyone."

"Yes I was there. I needed to see if you would turn up like my mum had predicted. I have always been a bit sceptical of what she says and her *all seeing eye*. Please don't tell her I said that. This time, I felt strongly about it and I wanted to believe. It felt so real, I did see you on the day of the fair and believe me, my heart skipped a beat. I couldn't make myself known. I didn't know how to, to be honest. I hope you can understand that, I didn't want to be upset, in case you didn't want to know me. I could feel your eyes staring after me, even when I had disappeared from your sight. I can only apologise. Will you accept my apology?"

"Yes of course. There is nothing to apologise for." Skye said.

"Tell me something", he continued, "About a month ago, I got this really weird feeling. Did you go to a certain concert and were you wearing the same perfume that you are wearing now?" he inhaled her aroma as he asked the last question.

"Oh my God, you *were* there. That's what you meant when I heard your voice say, *I will be* there."

Carl told Skye that he didn't remember shouting that out and it must have been during sleep, but he had been told the next morning by his mum, that he had been calling out.

"I got this feeling I was being watched, but the feeling I got when my favourite song came, it sent shivers down my spine. It was like my neck was being kissed gently up and down. It was a lovely feeling, but also kind of weird, if that makes sense." Skye commented.

"Yes that makes perfect sense. I was there although I didn't see you which was a shame. Believe it or not, I could feel a presence. I also got a similar feeling about an hour or so in to the concert. Mum says I have the gift as well and that we had both connected somehow."

Skye continued to look into his blue eyes and a smile appeared on her face. She took a step closer towards Carl. The rain was still falling on them as he touched her face and pulled her in, for that long awaited first kiss. It was soft and sensual just like the whispered voice had been. The chemistry just sparked between them. She didn't want the kiss to end, even though they were both getting soaked through to the skin now.

Skye eventually broke away from their kiss. Looking into his eyes, she tried to read his thoughts. If they were like hers, they were all of a blur. The last ten to fifteen minutes had been a blur.

"I think we should move out of the rain." Skye said. They stepped onto the steps of the waltzer which had a bit of a shelter.

They both smiled at each other and Carl started to speak again, "Now that I have finally found you, I don't want to let you go".

"I know how you feel. It has been a long time coming and to think I was about to give up hope. I thought it was all just a dream. I know that dreams do come true if you believe in them hard enough. The question now is, where do we go from here?" she said.

He leaned in and placed a single kiss on her forehead and said, "Well to start with, there is someone I want you to meet officially. Madam Rosa or Rose as she is normally known by her family and friends. To me she is just Mum".

Chapter 10

The warm summer rain had finally stopped. Thanks to the shelter of the waltzer, they were not completely soaked to the skin. Smiling at each other, they started to walk towards the refreshment stand. What Skye had not noticed earlier when she got a drink with her friends, or when she was walking through the empty fairground, was Madam Rosa's tent. It was just to the right of the refreshment stand, like it had been on the day of the psychic fair. Madam Rosa stood outside her tent smiling as Skye and Carl approached her.

She greeted Skye with a warm smile and a hug, whispering in her ear, "I knew you would find each other." Speaking aloud, she continued, "I am so pleased to meet you again officially this time. I wanted to tell you everything I knew when we first met. But I realised I had probably already said too much as it was. I think I scared you a little bit. I sincerely apologise and I hope you can find it in your heart to forgive a silly old fool like me".

Skye smiled at her and gave Madam Rosa a small kiss on the cheek. She turned back to Carl and placed her arms around his waist, "I know everything is going to be perfect from now on. I can feel it."

She could feel her whole body tingling as she rested her head on his shoulder, feeling the warmth of Carl's body as he held her tight, returning her hug.

Amber had walked over to Skye and Carl, and looked on in a slightly puzzled way.

"We thought you had gone back home." Amber said, "Is someone going to let me in, on what's happening here? Skye?"

"Amber, sorry I was a little longer than expected. This is Carl."

"Hello", he said as he leaned forward to shake Amber's hand.

"Hi," she said, still feeling a little confused, "Skye, do you want to elaborate a little more? Why don't I know anything about Carl?" Amber asked facing Skye.

"You could say myself and Carl have known each other for a while now. It has just taken us a little longer than expected to get here."

Carl looked at Skye and gave her a little wink. They both smiled at each other, knowing the private joke between them.

"I suppose it's time to introduce you to the rest of the gang. I can see the looks we are getting." Skye said to Carl as they started to walk towards the dodgems. Skye, Carl and Amber walked towards the rest of their friends. They were standing there, waiting and watching as the events slowly unfolded before them.

Skye introduced everyone to Carl. They invited him to join them on the dodgems. Now it was even and Skye didn't have to ride on her own. As Carl got into the car next to Skye, he looked over to his Mum. He gave her a wink and mouthed the words, *Thank you*.

The End

Coming Soon…

Her Guardian Angel by Sharon Atkinson

A supernatural romance novella

Being a guardian angel has its highs and lows, but for Dwight Fry, his latest assignment leaves him more confused than ever.

None of his previous assignments have ever been able to see him. That is until now. Faye has just turned 18 and not only can she see Dwight, she can also hear him.

Unsure of what his actual assignment is, Dwight and Faye embark on a journey to find out the truth and the reason why!

About the Author

Sharon has always been fascinated with the written word. As a writer, she writes poems straight from the heart and reflects this in order to inspire readers, with a different level of understanding and a feeling of the side that is not usually portrayed in your normal line of poems.

Since 2003 she has had 18 poems published in different anthologies including, "Poets of Greater London", "Love in Ink", "The Path of True Love" and "Daily Reflections 2005", to mention but a few. These have been published via ForwardPress. She also has her own collection of poems in "From Dreams to Reality" published by Authorhouse which came out in 2007 and Beyond Darkness: Deep, Dark & Romantic Poetry which was published via Createspace in 2015.

She has now started work on short stories and has two published in anthologies including "The Perfect Christmas Stuffing" and "No Sleeves and Short Dresses", both of which were to raise money for worthy causes.

She has completed her first novel, a Christmas romance, and has a few different projects in the pipeline.

Getting in touch:

If you wish to get in touch with Sharon Atkinson and find out what is on the horizon, please feel free to contact her via any of the following means. She promises she will always reply back to you.

Website: www.wordsandwoes.com

Twitter: @SharonSAtkinson

Email: Writingsharon@gmail.com

Acknowledgements

There are a few people that I should thank. Without whom, this probably would still be a rough story in one of my many notebooks.

Firstly, Monster for his continuous pushing me to keep writing (I personally think he is just after a new car and maybe a holiday from its profits ☺…). I keep hoping for that writing hut at the end of the garden!

To Sally Holtham for being their when I felt like pulling my hair out, when certain little bits would not go how I envisioned them. For being my rock and believing in me and for being a Beta Reader going through my work and helping me.

To Radka Louis and Amanda Paton, for agreeing to be my Beta Readers and making me delete half of my commas. Your input was extremely helpful and very much appreciated. I hope I have taken on board their opinions and shown it through this book.

Printed in Great Britain
by Amazon

45932560R00026